CALL ME TEACH

SJ SYLVIS

CALL ME TEACH

USA TODAY BESTSELLING AUTHOR

S.J. SYLVIS

ONE
NOLAN HUGHES AND HIS DIRTY SMIRK

HANNAH

"And then he told me that no one will be able to make me come the way he did."

Aria's mouth drops open. "I hope you told him that he's *never* made you come."

Her cheeks are red from anger, and mine are red from embarrassment. She blinks and waits for me to answer, but I come up empty-handed because if I had told him that, it wouldn't have been a lie. It's the truth. He never made me come and it wasn't because of him so much as it was because of me.

"Well?"

I shrug and stuff some more things into my bag.

"Hannah! You have to hit him where it hurts. His ego is everything, and to take a hit like that from you would be detrimental."

"And what about my ego?" I blow a loose piece of hair out of my face and push myself further back into the driver's seat, wishing it swallow me so I could end this conversation. Aria moves closer to her phone and eyes me with suspicion through the camera. I'm half tempted to hang up on her so I can avoid the whole thing altogether.

"I know that look." Her voice softens, and her pretty features smooth. She goes from angry to concerned in three seconds flat. "It's gonna be okay, Hannah. Your brother said you can live with him until I get there after the holidays. You did the right thing by ending it with Koa. He wasn't right for you."

I shake my head before she can carry on. "It wasn't him. It was me."

"Do not start that low-self-esteem bullshit with me, Hannah Evans!"

My throat grows tight, and my face burns hotter. "Aria, I think I'm broken."

Her cheeks pull tight with confusion as she waits for me to continue.

"I suck at sex."

She rolls her eyes. "With a body like yours? *Please.* Don't let your asshole ex make you feel like you're the problem, Hannah. Sometimes people just aren't meant to be together."

I climb out of my car with my phone in tow. I'm sure it's a very flattering angle with Aria staring up my nose, but I'm carrying one box and two bags, plus the phone, so she'll just have to deal.

I interrupt her uplifting sentiment. "That's not it." The front door closes behind me and I start the trek to my brother's floor. The apartment complex is less than five miles from Wilder U's campus, so at least I have that on my side. "It isn't just with Koa. It's with every guy."

"Wait...what?" Her voice echoes throughout the apartment hallway. "What do you mean?"

After putting my things on the floor, I lift the rug, pull

the spare key out from underneath it, and prepare myself for the scent of athletes to waft in my face when entering my new home. I already know I'm going to have to clean the apartment from ceiling to floor if I'm going to be able to handle living with hockey players that are probably just as untidy as the one I share DNA with.

"Well," I start, holding the door open with my foot while dragging a box in with one hand. "It's me. I'm the problem. And no..." I pause. "I am not quoting Taylor Swift. It's me. I haven't orgasmed with any guy! It's like I'm... broken or something!"

There's a loud commotion and I spin around in shock. Liquid sprays through the air, but even through the mist, I know it's not my brother who just overheard my very personal confession, causing their drink to jet from their mouth.

You've got to be fucking kidding me.

The blood drains from my face, and the phone drops from my hand with a loud clamor against the hardwood floor.

Aria is still chattering about my embarrassing divulgence, but instead of bending down and ending the call, I'm frozen. She goes on and on about different positions and tricks for me to orgasm the next time I'm getting "down and dirty with a guy".

Sweat begins to crest on the back of my neck and I pray for a piano to fall on my head.

Only it doesn't.

The only thing that falls is my heart because Nolan Huges is standing in front of me with a sexy smirk sliding onto his annoyingly handsome face.

TWO
HAYES'S SISTER, HAYES'S PROBLEM

NOLAN

I wipe the water from my mouth with the back of my hand and stare at a very frazzled—yet highly attractive—female standing in my living room with a face redder than my hockey jersey. My smirk deepens, and her lips part with a sweet gasp.

"Hello? Did you drop me? Are you hearing anything I'm saying?" The person on the phone sighs loudly. "It's as if *you're* the one in shock from telling me that you can't orgas—"

The girl scrambles to her knees in a rush and pushes end on the call at least fifteen times to silence her friend. I roll my lips together to keep myself from laughing at her expense and stare at her down below, on her knees.

Mmm, what a nice sight.

"Bro, I forgot to tell—"

I turn and face Hayes walking out of his bedroom, heading in my direction.

It all happens in slow motion. His haughty walk, the eye contact, and then *boom*. Down he goes, landing in the water that showered from my mouth because of the chick on the floor, who is currently drowning in her own embarrassment. It's kind of cute.

"What the fuck is on the floor?" Hayes growls.

I chuckle. "Besides you two? Water."

My roommate rises to his feet and swings his attention to the girl who is unmoving. "I thought you weren't coming until later?"

"And I thought you had practice." Her tone is snippy to say the least.

She's feisty, and hot.

Is this his girlfriend? Shouldn't he, like, help her up?

I would, but that would be crossing a line.

Instead of intervening, I round the counter and pour myself some more water. Thanks to Hayes, he mopped up the mess on the floor.

"Practice got pushed." he finally answers. "Why are you on the floor?"

I flick my eyes past the rim of my cup and watch the hottie shrug nonchalantly. "No reason. I prefer the ground."

I laugh and it echoes in my glass. Hayes ignores me but she doesn't. I catch her eye for a split second before she quickly looks away.

"Well good, 'cause that's where you'll be sleeping." Hayes says.

"Bro, what?" I can't help myself. "You're gonna make your girlfriend sleep on the floor?" What is his problem?

By the look of utter disgust on his face, I am fully aware that I've read the situation wrong. If she isn't his girlfriend, then who—

"Ew!" she shrieks, jumping to her feet.

Hayes pinches the bridge of his nose. "She's my sister, you sick fuck."

Sister? Oh shit.

"*This* is Hannah Banana?" My gaze sharpens on her.

Fuck me. She's...not what I expected. Hayes showed us her picture once. He didn't tell us that it was taken *at least* ten years ago.

I put my attention back to him. "I thought she was your younger sister."

"She is." he says.

I scoff. "Was the picture you showed us from third grade? Hannah Banana isn't ten years old! She's..." I look over at her, and she's sending me a death glare. "Our age!"

"Stop calling me Hannah Banana!" she hisses.

I pay her no mind because I'm going to call her whatever I want to call her.

Hayes throws his hands up. "If you guys knew she was our age and attended Wilder U, then I'd never hear the fucking end of it."

I chuckle. "You're leaving out a *very* important part of that sentence, and you know it."

She's hot, and the entire team is going to want to fuck her after they get wind. I understand his reasoning. I really do. What I don't understand is what she's doing in our apartment with a box of shit near her feet.

"What is she doing here?" I ask.

Hayes leans his hip against the counter. "That's what I wanted to talk to you about. She's going to be staying here for a few months until her friend starts the spring semester and they get their own apartment."

"And whose room is she staying in?" Because it sure as hell isn't going to be mine.

Hannah sighs loud enough to draw our attention. "Now I suddenly understand the floor comment."

That sucks for her.

A gentleman would offer up his bed but not when he plays for the hockey team and has the entire student body counting on him to win the season. I can't do that with lack of sleep and/or while sleeping on the floor myself.

I slowly walk around the counter, pass by Hayes, and then stop beside Hannah and her box of things. She stops breathing when I lean down into her space. "Good luck with the floor, Hannah Banana."

She growls and I smile like an asshole.

I lower my voice even more so her older brother won't hear. "And with the...*other* thing."

I move away before she can step on my foot and snag my keys so I can head to practice.

I don't mind that she's needing a place to stay. I'm hardly even here. You won't find me giving up my bed though.

Hayes's sister, Hayes's problem.

The floor will suit her just fine.

THREE
REMOTES MAKE GOOD WEAPONS

HANNAH

"On a scale of one to ten, how uncomfortable are you on that couch?" my brother asks on the way to the kitchen.

I adjust myself against the lumpy cushions and wince when he's out of sight. *This sucks.* "I'm half-tempted to move back in with Koa. That's how uncomfortable I am."

My brother peeks his head into the living room, which is now known as my bedroom. He narrows his gaze. "That's not funny."

I roll my eyes. "Don't act all protective now. If you *really* cared for me, you'd give up your bed."

His eyebrows dip. "I did, and you pretended to throw up."

I sit up taller and let my natural waves fall down my back. "Well, that's because I know what you do in your bed. There is no way I'm sleeping in it."

Gross.

Hayes snickers, but he doesn't disagree with me. I lived with him my entire life before he left for college. All my friends had crushes on him, and most of them didn't care to spare me the details if they ended up in a room with him at a party. I know entirely too much about my brother, and though I'm thankful he is giving me a place to stay to finish out the semester, it's less than ideal.

Not to mention, I can't even look his roommate in the face without feeling totally and utterly mortified. Every single time I see Nolan, I make a beeline in the other direction. That's how I met their—*my*—other roommate, Van.

I ran straight into his hard chest and fell backward onto my butt, which, ironically, was the second time I'd been on the floor in front of Nolan in less than a week.

Speak of the playboy.

"You can sleep in my room." Van walks into the living room and sits on the mismatched chair in the corner.

I knew he was my favorite. The only thing Nolan did was wish me good luck before he made a dig at my *other* bedroom problem.

Hayes shouts from the kitchen. "Not a chance, Van."

"He's right." Nolan says from down the hallway. "You need your rest just as much as the rest of the team."

My face begins to heat at the sound of his voice.

Van smirks, and I spy a little dimple on his cheek. "I'm one of the best players on the team. I'll be fine."

Hayes follows Nolan into the living room with a Chinese take-out container in his hand. "That wasn't my reason for saying no." My brother points his chopstick at Van. "I don't trust you with her."

I eye my brother closely. "What is that supposed to mean?"

Nolan moves to sit down on the couch, so I hurriedly pull my legs up to my chest so he doesn't smash them.

Doesn't he know this is my bed?

Instead of giving me any space, Nolan shifts and the

cushion dips, sending me closer to him. He raises an eyebrow. "It means he doesn't trust Van not to fuck you."

Van doesn't deny it. Instead, he just stares at me from across the room and shrugs.

"See!" Hayes shouts. "Stay away from her."

My face is warm.

As if I'd even consider sleeping with any of my brother's teammates. The hockey team is the talk of campus. I've heard too many stories about their wild escapades in the bedroom, and I'm not nearly confident enough to fake an orgasm with either of them. They'd see right through my feigned moans.

With Koa, it was different. He wasn't as adept in the bedroom. He probably didn't know the difference. But Nolan and Van would know right away.

A quick thought pops into my head that makes me blush harder. Would it be so bad to sleep with someone like them? Maybe they could teach me a thing or two.

I shake my head gently, then realize there are three sets of eyes on me. I start to sweat. "Can you guys leave? I'm tired."

"Or embarrassed."

I snap my gaze to Nolan and his half-crescent smile. "Why would I be embarrassed?"

I'm going to kick him.

He shrugs. "No reason."

Hayes looks between Nolan and me and finally settles on his best friend. "Why do I get a feeling that you know something I don't?"

My heart pounds as I stare at Nolan's strong, chiseled profile. He clears his throat, and when he opens his mouth, I ram my foot into the side of his tight torso. He whips his head over to me, and I send him a death glare. If he even considers telling my brother that I can't orgasm during sex, I will kill him in his sleep.

As if he can read my mind, he smirks before turning to my brother. "I know nothing. In fact, as of a few days ago, I thought your little sister was half your age."

I breathe a sigh of relief and go to move my foot out of his ribs. Shock ripples through my leg when Nolan's arm clamps down on it subtly, keeping it hostage.

"Well, she's not, and neither of you—along with the rest of the team—touches her. Got it?"

He's touching me right now.

Van stands. "Relax. We're not going to fuck your sister, Hayes."

"I'm literally right here," I say, flabbergasted.

Hayes ignores me and walks off behind Van to their own bedrooms.

I try to pull my foot away again, but Nolan keeps it in its place, trapped beneath his arm. Our eyes meet, and he raises an eyebrow. *God, it should be illegal to be that attractive.*

"I saw that look."

My pulse skips. "What look?"

He flashes his white teeth in my direction. "I saw the wheels turning. You want one of us to fuck you, don't you?"

My lips part with shock. His eyes zero in on my mouth.

"Excuse me?" I act completely appalled with his accusation, but *damn.* He's right. The thought crossed my mind, and it's scary that he knew. It just proves that he'd see through my fake orgasm like I'd already assumed.

"I could be wrong, but your eyes lit up when your brother was accusing Van of wanting to fuck you."

"That is not true." I argue.

"It wouldn't be a bad idea." Nolan stretches his legs out

in front of him, seeming to relax. "Maybe then you could orgasm during sex."

That's it. I'm going to kill him in his sleep.

He just *had* to bring it up.

"That conversation was not for you." I pull forcefully on my leg, and he lets it go.

He chuckles before climbing to his feet. He stretches his arms above his head and his t-shirt rides up, showing off his toned stomach. "I know," he says, glancing at me. "But I still heard it."

My ears burn as I watch him walk away. Before he gets too far, he turns and sends me a flirty look. "I'm just saying, maybe you're sleeping with the wrong guys if they can't get you off—"

I pick up the remote and throw it at him. He ducks, and I miss him by an inch. When he pops back up, his smile is annoyingly contagious. "Night, Hannah Banana."

Then he winks, and I fly back onto the lumpy couch and try to think of anything but sleeping with either of my brother's teammates.

FOUR
HOCKEY IS BETTER THAN FOOTBALL

NOLAN

My dick twitches when a familiar fruity scent floats down the hallway and under my closed door. Not even a lengthy hockey practice and ethics paper could tire me out with Hayes's sister showering no less than a few yards from my bedroom.

She's naked in there.

I sit up in my bed and sigh with my head turned toward the sound of water hitting the tiles. As soon as the shower cuts off, I silently thank God and flop backward. It's no more than a few minutes later when I hear her bare feet pattering against the hardwood floor and her soft voice carrying on a conversation.

"I mean, he had a point. But I can't take him up on his offer. It's not like I can sleep with him."

He? If one of the guys on the team is trying to make moves on Hayes's sister, he's going to go ballistic. Shortly after the team got wind that his sister is staying in our apartment and that she isn't hard on the eyes, the jokes started, and Hayes's forehead vein made an appearance.

Hannah Evans is off-limits.

I swing my legs off the side of my bed and walk over to my door. I have great deductive skills, and I'll know which teammate is signing his own death wish before I even make eye contact with Hannah. Then I'll be forced to put a stop to it before Hayes gets thrown off the team for fighting.

I'm prowling down the hallway like a creep, sniffing the air like I've never smelled a freshly showered woman before, and I come to a halt to listen.

"I've done some research." *That's Hannah's friend on the phone.* "Reign Kendrix."

The quarterback?

"No way," Hannah's voice squeaks.

I should go back to my room. It's confirmed the *he* they were referring to has nothing to do with the hockey team, but nonetheless, my feet stay planted on the floor, and I listen some more.

"Why not?"

Hannah scoffs. "He's like a god on campus. There is no way I'm going to date him just so I can become a little more skilled in the bedroom. He'll probably sleep with me once and then ghost me." She pauses. "If he would even consider dating me. I'm not setting myself up for failure, Aria. I'm already self-conscious."

"Then maybe you should ask Nolan." I straighten my spine. *Excuse me?* "He was the one who came up with the idea. I bet he'd be down to fuck."

Suddenly, I become extremely invested in Hannah's response. What does Hayes's little sister actually think about me when I'm not around? Because when I'm within distance, she either sends me a scathing look or blushes. I can't quite figure her out.

"Ooh!" her friend exclaims loudly, and Hannah shushes

her. "What if Nolan just helps you in the bedroom! Like, gives you some lessons, and *then* you go on a date with Reign. Who knows what'll come from it?"

"That's..." Hannah sounds appalled by the idea but then she pauses. "Nolan would never go for that. He was half-kidding. Plus, that's a terrible idea. What would I say to him? 'Hey, Nolan... Do you think you could teach me how to orgasm during sex so I can stop sucking in the bedroom and maybe someday I'll be able to enjoy a relationship?'"

My heart starts to beat faster at the prospect, and although it's wrong on every ethical level, I put a toe forward and make myself known.

Hannah drops the phone in her lap and stares at me with wide eyes. Her heart-shaped mouth opens, and a shocked noise flies out. I raise an eyebrow and pride myself on my toned stomach, because she drops her gaze to my shirtless torso and flushes harder.

"That's exactly what you could say." I'm as smooth as they come, and she knows it.

"Is that Nolan?!" Her friend's voice is muffled from the blanket that Hannah has draped over her lap, but she disappears altogether when Hannah ends the video call.

"Again with the eavesdropping!" she snaps. Her cheeks are bright, and I fucking love that I make her uncomfortable.

I keep my attention pinned to her while walking closer to the couch she's been sleeping on. She doesn't take a breath until I'm standing a foot away, peering down at her. I can't help but grab onto her chin tightly and angle her face to look at me. "Well?"

"Well what?" she whispers.

"You gonna ask me or what?"

Her gulp catches my attention, and so does my flickering pulse.

I'll admit it; I'm attracted to her. She's hot, and her attitude with me is an irresistible temptation. She won't say yes, which is exactly why I'm toying with her.

After a few seconds of our gazes locked, she hastily crosses her arms and puts her nose in the air. "I rather chew my arm off than ask you to help me."

I spy a lie. She won't look me in the eye and her cheeks turn the prettiest shade of pink.

I drop my hand and chuckle deeply. She glares at me as I causally walk backwards. "You know where I am when you change your mind."

I turn and she scoffs.

"I'm not going to change my mind." she states.

Probably not, but it's fun to entertain the idea all the same.

FIVE
LIKE BROTHER, LIKE SISTER

NOLAN

Hayes is going to lose his shit.

We have one rule at the apartment, and it's *no parties*.

Tell me why Van has a plethora of people surrounding him in the living room with music spilling out of the Bluetooth speaker and multiple bottles of hard liquor laid out.

"Bro, really?" I rest my palms against the counter. "What are all these people doing here?"

He smirks. "Celebrating."

"Celebrating what?" I slide my gaze to the blonde on the couch who keeps staring at me.

Van pauses, and I bring my attention back to him. He thinks for a moment and then shrugs. "Life?"

I snicker and reach for something less potent than the vodka and tequila. "Hayes is going to kill you. You know he hates parties."

Van rolls his eyes and grabs a bottle. "Hayes is at the library, getting tutored by some nerd he secretly wants to fuck between the aisles of books. He won't be home for a while."

As if on cue, the front door opens.

I prepare for Hayes to immediately throw everyone out the second he walks into the living room, but to my surprise, it's not Hayes.

It's our other roomie: Hannah.

"Hannah!" Van strides over to her and throws his arm around her shoulders. Confusion blankets her face until she eyes all the alcohol laid out and multiple people in the living room—also known as her bedroom.

My lips roll together to suppress a laugh.

Like brother, like sister. Hannah huffs with anger, and the apples of her cheeks turn red.

"Van! I thought there was a house rule of no parties?!" Her arms cross against her jacket. She looks to me for help, but the only thing I do is tip my beer back and take a swig.

"This isn't a party." He's nonchalant. "Don't tell me you've never been to a real party, Hannah Banana."

I watch her closely. Her eyes narrow with annoyance, and I can't help but feel slightly excited by it.

My beer bottle clanks when I place it back on the counter, pulling her attention to me versus Van—something I'm sort of....pleased with?

"I don't think she knows how to party," I say casually. "I mean, she doesn't even know how to..." I let my sentence linger.

Hannah's spine straightens.

I smile.

She knows exactly what I was about to say. No one else has any idea...but she does.

Her hefty sigh travels all the way across the open space and hits me right in the face. She flings Van's arm from her shoulders and heads right for me.

"You're a dick," she whispers, leaning extra close to me.

I'm really not a dick, but it's too much fun to poke at her.

"No"—I lean in closer—"but I do have one that you can use if you want."

She gasps, and I chuckle.

"Relax, Hannah Banana. I'm just fucking you."

Her face flames.

"I mean...I'm just fucking *with* you."

Her tiny growl is music to my ears.

Why is this so fun?

When she pulls back, I catch a quick glimpse of her pretty blue eyes. Something digs itself into my stomach that I can't ignore.

Sure, I'm just messing around with her, but I can't pretend the attraction isn't there. There's a part of me that wonders if I really could help her.

It sort of feels like a challenge.

Can I be the one to get Hayes's sister to orgasm? I've never had issues getting a girl to come, so who's to say I can't help her?

I blink a few times to clear my thoughts and realize that Hannah has stolen my beer and is halfway to the living room with Van's arm around her shoulders again.

What the hell?

"Van," I warn from the kitchen. "Hayes will kill you for the party and then bring you back to life just to kill you again for touching his sister."

"You're Hayes's sister?" some guy I don't recognize asks.

His eyes grow wide when Hannah nods.

I raise an eyebrow when he glances at me.

Don't even think about it.

I catch the way his lip lifts, like he's just waiting for me to disappear before trying something with her, which means I'll have to partake in the socializing—at least until Hayes gets home—because even though this entire thing is Van's doing, I'll probably get some of the blame too.

SIX
HE KNOWS MY DIRTY LITTLE SECRET

HANNAH

I'm uncomfortable.

I've been to college parties before, but the fact that random people are sitting on my *bed,* and I can't just disappear into my own room to get away from them, makes me tense—something that Nolan can't seem to stop pointing out.

He's been teasing me since I walked in the door, and I'm seconds from going into his room to sleep and leaving him out here for the rest of the night.

"So, Hayes's sister..."

I swing my attention to Saint. He introduced himself to me three seconds after Van pulled me into the living room.

"I have a name," I say softly, trying not to be a bitch.

His cheek lifts. "Hannah."

At least he remembered it.

"You got a boyfriend?"

Nolan snorts from the other end of the living room. I swing my gaze to him, and he's staring right at me. His eyebrow hitches, as if he's wanting to see how this entire thing plays out.

I know it's only because he knows my dirty little secret, and to be honest, it's kind of pissing me off a little.

An idea pops into my head. It's a bad idea—one that will make my brother irate, and Nolan too, so I choose to ignore it.

I sip on my mixed drink and force myself to keep my face smooth, even though the bitter taste of vodka makes me want to vomit right in Saint's lap.

"I don't have a boyfriend," I finally say, pulling my attention back to the hotshot baseball player.

Apparently, Saint is one of the top baseball players in college right now—something he humbly disagreed with when brought up.

"No boyfriend?" There's a twinkle in his eye, and I can't help but play along.

"Nope," I say, letting the word plop out of my mouth.

Saint smiles at me before pulling his beer up to his lips. He's super hot. Too hot for me. I know he's experienced. It's written all over his devious grin and bedroom eyes.

"Are you looking for a boyfriend?" he asks, scooting a little closer to me on the couch.

I lower my voice after briefly catching Nolan's eye. *Stop looking at me like that.*

"Not really." I stare into Saint's eyes for a quick second and then drop my attention to his mouth.

His tongue jolts out between his lips and wets them. "Want to go somewhere else and talk? Van won't shut the hell up."

A laugh leaves me. He's right. Van is tipsy and loud.

"Uh..." I impulsively flick my gaze to Nolan. He

narrows his eyes and grins, and it does nothing but fuel my bad idea.

"You know what?" 3, 2, 1. "Sure. Follow me."

I stand on steady feet, and Saint, pleased beyond belief, does the same. My hand falls to his, and I keep my back to Nolan the entire time, because I already know he's watching my every move.

Van's loud voice is beginning to disappear the farther we get down the hallway. I place my palm on Nolan's bedroom door and turn the knob with my heart racing.

I expect Nolan to come rushing after us, especially since he has a direct line to the hallway and can likely see me entering *his* room with Saint, but to my surprise, he doesn't follow.

The door latches behind me, and Saint's hands fall to my hips.

"Alone at last," he whispers, gently pushing me against the wall beside the door. Then he kisses me, and I realize right away that I've made a grave mistake.

SEVEN
ALL YOU HAVE TO DO IS ASK

NOLAN

No girl has ever made my heart beat this fast, and to think, Hannah isn't even outright doing anything to me.

Or is she?

Watching her lead Saint by the hand down the hall and disappearing behind *my* bedroom door has me in a frenzy. I can't decide if she did it on purpose because I was teasing her, or for some other reason.

It doesn't take a genius to figure out what they're doing in my room, and it doesn't take much to pull me that direction.

The longer I sit back with a beer in my hand and some blonde by my side, the more invested in Hannah I become.

She's hard to figure out.

The blonde beside me isn't.

"I'll be right back," I say, patting the blonde's thigh.

I haul myself up after Van turns his back away from me and walk casually down the hallway. A deep breath escapes and I turn the door knob slowly. I press on the door when it unlatches and silently enter my bedroom. Neither Hannah nor Saint are aware of my presence, and I stand back and watch as he tongue fucks her against the wall of my bedroom.

A sense of urgency rushes through me, like I want to pull him away from her.

I blame it on the fact that Hayes is my bestfriend and since he isn't here, it's my responsibility to *protect* his little sister, but my dick argues with that point.

The way Hannah kisses Saint back sends a shiver down my spine. Saint has one hand wrapped around her lower back and the other falls to her leg. He brings it up and traps it around his back, giving him all the room to dry hump Hayes's sister against my bedroom wall.

That's enough.

I clear my throat and Hannah breaks the kiss. *Good girl.*

Her flushed face tilts past Saint's shoulder and our eyes clash. I raise an eyebrow and the relief I see is enough to throw Saint out.

"Out."

Saint doesn't let go of Hannah and I pretend like it doesn't bother me.

"Bro, what?" he says over his shoulder.

I chuckle and try to play off my irritation. "This is my room. Hannah Banana here brought you here just to piss me off."

She makes a pouty noise. "Where else am I supposed to go? It's not like I have my own room."

"We can go back to my place." Saint says, turning away from me.

My stomach dips with the thought of her going with him. Do I suddenly want Hayes's sister? Why do I care?

"Um," Hannah's voice is soft and hesitant.

Before she can answer, the music in the living room cuts off and her brother's voice cuts through the air.

"Everyone out."

Hannah's shoulders drop with relief.

"Sorry," she says. "Big brother is home and there's no way he's letting me leave with you."

Saint growls silently but eventually lets her leg fall. He pulls out his phone and tells her to put her number in there, all while I stand back half-amused at the exchange. The other half is not so amused.

"Later." Saint flicks his chin to me and begins to walk out of the room with Hannah following closely behind.

I wait until she thinks she's in the clear before wrapping my hand around her delicate wrist to pull her backwards into my room.

My dick jolts with her hot gasp, but I bypass that and smirk when she glares at me.

"You're welcome." I say.

Her perfect bow-shaped lips part. "Excuse me?"

Oh, we're going to play coy?

I lean down, putting my face close to hers. "I said... you're welcome."

Her chin tilts. "For?"

"For saving you when your plan backfired."

Seeing the truth flash across her face makes me grin.

"Don't act like you were bringing Saint in here just so he'd fuck you when we both know you were only doing it to make me angry." *And it sort of worked.*

Hannah's arms cross against her chest and I know she's about to argue with me. I take her by surprise when I grip the side of her face and plunge my fingers through her hair.

"I saw the relief on your face the second I cleared my

throat in the room, Hannah. If you want my help learning how to orgasm during sex, all you have to do is ask."

I'm prepared for her to stomp on my foot, or at the very least, for her to scoff, but she surprises me when her teeth sink into her bottom lip and those pretty blue eyes soften with vulnerability.

"If I ask, are you going to say yes?"

Aw, fuck. I wasn't expecting that. But I'm not one to back down from a challenge, so I throw her my best smirk. "I'll help you, Hannah Banana." *This isn't a good idea.* "But we've gotta keep it a secret. Your brother put a no-touch rule on you, and he's not only my teammate and roommate, but my friend too. It goes against the code."

Heavy silence lingers between us so I try to lighten the mood. "But this means you owe me. You know that, right?"

She rolls her eyes and I slowly untangle my fingers from her hair. I open my door further and peek down the hall to make sure Hayes isn't within sight.

"I owe you? Like a favor? What kind of favor?" Hannah is rambling, and it's kind of cute.

I flick my chin to the hall, silently telling her it's safe to leave my room before Hayes figures out that she was in here. When there's a proper amount of distance between us, the threshold of my room being our only barrier, I shrug. "I'll let you know whenever I figure it out."

The door is almost fully closed when I hear her whisper-shout. "I won't do your homework for you, Nolan!"

I chuckle.

As if I need her for her brains.

EIGHT
I'M NOT CALLING HIM TEACH

HANNAH

I can hardly look him in the eye.

My brother is oblivious to my nerves, but Nolan isn't. His long fingers tap against the counter as Hayes continues the conversation about my ex-boyfriend that makes me highly uncomfortable, especially with Nolan actively listening.

At least he isn't eavesdropping this time, but *still*.

"Dad said he owed me one," Hayes says in between a bite of pizza.

"For what?" I'm half afraid to know the answer.

"For getting you away from Koa."

Nolan is staring at me. I can feel his eyes on me like a hot, searing brand.

"I got myself away from Koa." My response is fueled with annoyance. "And I thought they liked him?"

Hayes snickers. "He treated you like shit."

I frown. "They didn't know that, though."

He mumbles under his breath before finishing his pizza. "They do now."

I yell at his backside as he quickly heads for the door. "Hayes!"

"Sorry, I can't hear you!" he shouts just before the lock clicks.

Not only has my brother just carelessly humiliated me in front of Nolan, but he's also left me alone with him for the first time since he offered himself up as tribute to help me in the bedroom.

I'm already on edge and embarrassed. The very last thing I want to do is turn around and face him now, but he clears his throat, and I know it's my cue.

I spin on my heels, and we immediately make eye contact. My pulse skips, and although I didn't think it was possible, I suddenly feel even less confident than before. His fingers are tapping again, and it sets my nerves on fire.

"So," he starts, "not only could your ex not decipher a fake orgasm from a real one, but he also treated you poorly?" He hums under his breath when I don't answer. "What exactly did he do that was so bad, besides not getting you off, Hannah Banana?"

I'm hot all over, and I try to channel my emotions into anger. "Well, at least he didn't call me by my childhood nickname..."

I get a quick peek at Nolan's white teeth when he lifts a lip. "You don't like my nickname for you. Noted."

A heavy sigh leaves the pit of my stomach. Getting spicy lessons from my brother's roommate and star player of Wilder U's hockey team is a terrible idea. It's not going to work. I'm already uncomfortable with his eyes on me from across the room, let alone if I surrender to his touch.

I start to walk past the kitchen counter that Nolan is leaning against with defeat cheering me on. Being intimate with someone is a very vulnerable thing to do, and unfortunately, vulnerability and Hannah do not go well together. That's *exactly* why this isn't going to work.

"Not so fast." Nolan's hand wraps around my waist, and he spins me until I'm pressed against his hard chest.

I gulp when he refuses to let me go. He bounces those greenish-blue eyes in between mine and tilts his head. "Where do you think you're going?"

"To my…" *Shit, I don't have a bedroom here.*

"To avoid me some more? I thought you wanted my help?" He flicks an eyebrow, and somehow, that small gesture makes him ten times more attractive.

I push off his chest, but he keeps me trapped. "It's not going to work."

"Why not?" he asks.

I roll my eyes. "Because you're you, and I'm me! That's why."

He thinks for a moment. "What is that supposed to mean?"

I stare at the fridge behind him so I can force the words out of my mouth. "You make me…" *This is so embarrassing.* "Uneasy."

Nolan pulls back slightly, and I swing my eyes past his shoulder to see his reaction. He's looking at me very closely, and I'm pretty sure I have hives breaking out along my skin.

"Let's go." He grips my wrist and drags me down the hallway. My attempt at putting the brakes on is pitiful. Nolan continues to tug until we're outside his bedroom door.

"I told you this isn't going to work. What are you doing?" My heart beats a little faster when he turns the knob and pushes me inside. I immediately look at his bed and feel something twist in my lower belly.

When the door shuts, I turn, and our gazes collide.

"They don't call me *Teach* for nothing, Hannah." Nolan runs a deft hand through his unruly hair. "Now get on the bed."

NINE
WILL SOMEONE TURN THE LIGHTS BACK ON?

NOLAN

I've been thinking of nothing except hockey and watching Hayes's sister come apart in front of my eyes. However, I'll admit that I pictured my fingers helping her get there, but I've had to rethink my lessons after watching her cute cheeks heat from embarrassment.

"Now, Hannah." There's an edge to my voice that she notices. She flips her long, thick hair over her shoulder and pulls back slightly.

I take a step toward her, and she takes one back. We do this until she falls onto my bed.

"Thank you," I say.

Hannah's pink lips purse, and I already know she's about to reiterate her refusal, so I put my hand up to stop her.

"I get it. I make you a little uneasy. I have a reputation that I'm sure you've heard of, and it's clear that I'm the one with experience here." Her gaze darts away, and it kind of bothers me that she's so embarrassed by that. "There's nothing wrong with not fully knowing your own body,

Hannah. It's obvious no one has given you the chance to explore what you like in the bedroom, which only drives the point further that your ex *was* a piece of shit. Maybe every ex, if it's true what you said."

She swallows loudly.

"It is, isn't it? You've never gotten off during sex?"

She turns away instead of answering. I sigh and reach down to turn her attention back to me.

"Lesson number one," I start. "You have to get comfortable with me if this is going to work. Stop being embarrassed and self-conscious."

"And how do you expect me to do that?" She's peering up at me with her baby blues, and a swift feeling of guilt whips through me because I have a feeling that I'm going to enjoy this way too much. Not to mention, it's behind Hayes's back.

"Well..." I lightly push on her shoulders, and she falls back onto my bed. It's a sight that I admittedly enjoy, even with the guilt lingering. I bite my lower lip as I caress her body with my gaze. "I'm gonna watch you get off on my bed. All on your own, baby."

Hannah pops up quickly, her chestnut hair whizzing past her face. "No way."

"Yes way." I lean down and push her back onto the mattress. "You have to get comfortable with me, Hannah. And yourself."

"I am comfortable with myself." It's obvious that she's angry by the way she crosses her arms over her perky chest. I'm silently cursing her tight leggings because they show off every inch of her curves, and I'm going to spend the rest of the night wondering what she looks like beneath the fabric if she doesn't do this.

"Are you, though?" I move over to my desk chair, turn it

around, and take a seat. I lean forward with my elbows on my knees. "If you're so comfortable with yourself, why won't you show me?"

She mumbles under her breath.

"If you're going to insult me, at least do it so I can hear you."

"I'm not insulting you," she says louder this time. "I'm just wondering what is in this for you. Maybe I'm wondering if you have some ulterior motive for helping me."

"No ulterior motive. I just like when people owe me favors." Not to mention, I *love* a challenge.

"What kind of favors?" Her question falls out of her mouth slowly. She's hesitant, so I throw her a bone.

"If another puck bunny tries to pin me for something I didn't do, you can be my alibi."

"A puck bunny tried to pin you for something before?"

I nod. "It was a rumor—one that I killed almost instantly with camera footage. I was nowhere near her, but she tried to get back at me for turning her down and created some elaborate story to get me kicked off the hockey team."

All it takes is one refusal for a date and I'm suddenly in deep shit because someone got their feelings hurt. It would be nice to have a backup plan.

"Are you in or not?" I'm becoming impatient, and it won't be too long before Hayes comes home, and then our time alone will be gone.

Hannah's lips roll together, and she flops back onto my bed, sending her sugary scent billowing into the open space. My nostrils flare.

"Can we...at least turn the lights off?"

I stare at her rising chest and can practically feel the nerves rolling off her. I grip the arms of my chair before rising to my feet and walking over to the light switch. The room is pitch black now, but it doesn't take long to adjust to the darkness. Her shadow on my bed is the only thing I'm looking at as I make my way back to the chair.

"Alright, Hannah. Let's see what you've got."

She mumbles under her breath, but I can see her hands playing with the waistband of her leggings before they're shoved past her waist.

A hot swallow works its way down my throat.

"Lock the door, Nolan."

Yes, ma'am.

TEN
I'M THE TEACHER. YOU'RE THE STUDENT

HANNAH

The locking of the door sends my pulse jumping. Nerves itch my flesh, but there's a bubble of anticipation in my lower belly that forces my hand to move over my hip bone.

"Since I can't see you, I need you to tell me what you're doing to yourself. I need to know what you like."

My nipples harden at the sound of Nolan's smooth voice from the corner of his bedroom. I open my mouth to talk, but I'm hit with a blinding shyness. "I... I can't." *What am I supposed to say?*

"You can, and you will." He pauses. "Or I'll just turn the lights on and watch you."

I smash my lips together at his brash demand. Nolan is charismatic, and his bright smile is contagious, but hearing him make demands of me in the bedroom is downright provocative. His voice is hot.

"Where are your hands, Hannah?"

A rush of heat wraps around my neck, but I manage to speak. "One is on my hip, and the other is on my thigh."

"Okay, now if I weren't in this room with you, where would you be putting those hands?"

I swallow and lick my lips. "Um..."

"Do it, and then tell me."

A breathy sigh leaves my mouth, but I do what he says. I'm afraid I'll freak out at the last second and be too shy to actually get myself off, like in the past, but there's a deep yearning inside that makes me *want* to do this in front of him. It's a scandalous thought, and I run with it because, for the first time, I don't feel like I'm about to hit a wall.

"Bet–between my legs," I whisper.

"Both hands?" There's a hoarseness present in Nolan's voice that I notice right away.

I creep one hand up my shirt and underneath my bra.

"Just one."

"And where is the other?"

"Up my shirt."

He hums, and I swear I can feel the vibration against my skin. "So you like to be touched all over. That's good to know."

I breathe faster when he talks. I slip a finger under the top of my panties and subtly gasp from the featherlight touch against my clit.

"I can hear you getting worked up. Talk to me, Hannah."

I shut my eyes even though it's already dark in the room. "What do you want to know, Nolan?"

There's a shifting in the corner of the room, and I imagine him walking over to me and taking over. I picture him taking one of my hands and pinning it to the bed while he replaces my finger with his. I've seen him on the ice. I know how confident he is and how he holds his hockey stick with a steady grip. I'm certain he'd be good with his hands.

"What are you thinking about as you touch yourself? Where does your mind go when you're all alone, baby?"

Another quiet gasp spills from my mouth. I push a finger inside and take my other hand and start rubbing circles against my clit. All while picturing *him*.

"Hannah." Nolan's voice is closer, but I'm too invested in the pleasure. "Tell me, or I won't let you get off."

I half-laugh. "Like you could stop me now."

My eyes fly open when I feel his tight grip on my wrist. The room is still near black, but Nolan's body heat wafts over me as he holds me captive. "I'm the teacher. You're the student. You have to obey."

Sweat pricks my scalp, and my breathing is labored. I try to tug on my hand, but Nolan's fingers tighten. "I'm waiting, Hannah. Tell me what you think about when you're alone. I wanna know the things your dirty little mind conjures up."

Oh my god.

I tug again, and he laughs.

"Fine!" I blurt. "I was thinking about you."

For a moment, everything stops. His breathing, my breathing, the tight grip on my wrist.

"Good girl," he whispers, lessening his hold. "Now earn your A..."

He gently pushes my hand farther down, and I arch my back when my finger goes deeper. My teeth sink into my lower lip when he whispers in my ear.

"Next time, I'm the one that gets to feel you come against my fingers, though."

A hot sensation rushes everywhere, and my whimper is loud enough to make my cheeks burn. His hand remains wrapped around my wrist as I move my finger in and out, relishing in the feeling.

"You must be getting close," he grits. "You're getting louder."

I want to tell him to shut up so I don't get distracted but for some reason, Nolan's voice does the opposite. It pulls me in deeper and blinds me with even more pleasure.

When his teeth skim my neck, I gasp and realize that it's *game over*. I come fast and hard, and it takes me too long to regain consciousness. When I finally pull my hands out of my panties, I nearly come again because Nolan does something that no man has ever done before.

He takes my wrist, pulls my hand up to his mouth, and licks the length of my finger.

I feel his smirk against my palm.

"I'm going to make you come with my mouth too."

I'm silenced by his dirty talk.

He lies beside on me on the bed and even though we're no longer touching, I feel him everywhere.

"Has anyone gotten you off like that before?" he asks.

I shake my head, even though I know he can barely see me.

"Good," he whispers before getting off the bed and opening his bedroom door.

There's a sliver of light from the hallway shining into his room, giving us both the perfect window to each other. Our eyes meet, and the hunger I see in his gaze makes my stomach bottom out.

"I gotta go take care of something." His throat bobs. "Meet me at the rink Monday night. 9pm."

I'm met with an empty doorway a second later.

Then I hear the bathroom door shut, and the shower kicks on.

I suddenly understand what he has to take care of, and

the confidence it gives me is enough to put a smile on my face.

ELEVEN
WATCH AND LEARN

NOLAN

I'm spent.

My body is tired, and my arms ache from the number of assists I shot to Hayes during practice.

We have a game in two days, and Coach is making sure we're ready.

With all that said, it still isn't stopping the anticipation backing my every step to the empty stands.

The rest of the team has left, and the thought of being alone in this big ol' arena with Hayes's sister is hotter than I will admit. I've been thinking of nothing but her little moan from last weekend. My eyes have been following her every movement around the apartment—even with her brother in the room. It's kind of putting me in a bad position because it's not like I can just ask his permission to fuck her. It's not like I want to take her on a date and treat her with respect. Instead, I want to watch her come all over my hand and then stick my dick inside of her to get her off *again*. And for what? I guess for her to try things out on some stupid football jock, but whatever.

I pause at the doorway when I see her standing in the bottom row, right next to the sin bin. Her back is to me with her long, warm-colored chestnut hair spilling down her back. My first thought is how perfect her locks are for pulling, but then I backpedal when the word beautiful comes to mind.

She truly is beautiful. I'm not sure I've ever thought of the opposite sex like that before. I know an attractive woman when I see one, but Hannah is different. Maybe it's because I see her in her element, when she thinks no one is watching, or that I've seen her without any makeup on, sleeping peacefully on the couch. Either way, she is more than hot.

I shake my head and leisurely walk down the rest of the steps until I'm right beside her. She glances at me for a split second before turning back to the empty rink.

"Why did you have me meet you here?" she asks.

My elbow brushes hers, and I feel the energy already simmering between us. *Fuck, we have chemistry.* "Because Hayes will be home tonight, and I don't think he'll appreciate hearing his sister moan from my bedroom."

I smirk when she snaps her head to me. Her jaw is unhinged, and I get a quick look at her straight teeth. She quickly crosses her arms, and I know she's about to hit me with a bratty remark. "So confident in thinking you'll be the one to get me to moan."

See? Brat.

I side-eye her, and it shuts her up. My hands are on her hips a breath later, and I spin her around before forcefully pushing her up against the glass. "Want to try that again, Hannah Banana?" We both swallow at the same time, and it's obvious to me that she feels the heat between us too. "I can tease you until you're begging me to fuck you, and I promise I'll be able to get you off." I pause. "That's not to say I will, though."

Her bottom lip disappears behind her teeth, and there's a little voice in the back of my head that is begging for me to kiss her.

I'm not much of a kisser. I'll suck on a girl's neck, pull on her lobe with my teeth, and whisper dirty things into her ear, but I'm not a big fan of making out. It's too...intimate.

But I kind of want to kiss her right now.

"Fine." She finally breaks. "What's the lesson for tonight, then?"

Excitement nearly chokes me. I grip her hips tighter to keep her steady because I have a feeling she wants to flee. "I'm gonna watch you get off under the lights."

Her lips part. "What?"

I nod. "You did it for me in the dark, and now you're going to do it where I can watch."

Her eyes fall to my chest, and I'm thankful she can't see how fast my heart is beating.

"It's a lesson that needs to be learned, Hannah. You can't be embarrassed. The sooner you're comfortable with showing me what you look like when you come, the sooner you'll be able to do it during sex." She meets my eye for a brief second because she knows I'm right. "I think that's your problem. You are afraid to let anyone see you like that. You're afraid to give someone the power to bring you to the brink and then watch you break."

She's looking everywhere but at my face, and suddenly, this isn't about getting her skills up to par in the bedroom and more about proving to her that she can be vulnerable with me. I want to make her feel safe enough to let me see her like that.

Fuck, what am I getting myself into?

"Before you get off for me," I say, removing my hands from her waist. "I want to show you something." I pull her toward the locker room. Once we're inside and the door is shut, I take her to the bench that has the perfect view of the showers. "Take a seat. I'm going to get off for you first."

Her mouth opens in shock, but to my surprise, she takes a seat.

"Good girl," I say before stripping off my shirt and throwing it to the side. "Now watch and learn."

TWELVE
IF YOU WANT SOMETHING, TAKE IT

HANNAH

Steam billows out from the shower, and I'm already sweating. My teeth clamp down against one another when Nolan grips the waistband of his joggers and drops them to his ankles. I immediately skip my attention past his defined abs and lock onto the grip he has on himself.

Oh my god...

I'm not a virgin, but looking at a naked Nolan makes me feel like I am.

His bare feet slap against the wet tile, and I stare at the rippling muscles along his spine. They flicker when he reaches up and runs his hand through his damp hair. Heat hits me in the face when he turns slightly, and I get a glimpse of his strong profile. *He's perfect.*

"You okay over there?" Water drips to the edge of his nose, and he flicks his head. He turns all the way around and grips himself again.

I swallow and nod, although my throat is slowly closing.

"Can you see okay, Hannah?" His question is a tease, and I feel it in between my legs.

"Yes," I whisper, dropping my attention from his face to his moving hand. He was already hard when he stripped, but somehow, he's even harder. His dick makes his hand look small, but there is nothing small about Nolan. He's six feet three inches tall, and there isn't a muscle on his body that isn't painted with strength.

"This is what it's like to feel fully confident, babe." His hand moves up and down as he continues to milk himself, and there's a well-known throb in my core. "I like you watching me," he admits.

"You do?" I ask in complete awe.

"I fucking love it. It's hot watching you watch me."

His head flings backward, and his jaw slacks with pleasure.

I stand up because I can't sit any longer. My chest heaves with something intense, and I bite my lip harder when he moves his hand up and down at a pace that has me imagining all sorts of dirty things. Our eyes catch, and he raises an eyebrow after flinging the water from his face off into the distance.

"Hannah..." My name is strained coming from his mouth. "If you want something, take it."

It's like he just summoned me somehow.

I erase the distance between us, and although I'm fully dressed, I let the warm water pelt me from above. I grab onto him and take over.

"Fuck," he mutters.

His hold on my wrist pushes me to go faster. I grip him hard, and pleasure courses through my veins. I have never wanted to please a man to this extent before. It always felt like a job to me, a task that had no reward at the end, but watching Nolan completely lose himself is enough to feed my dirty thoughts for years. "Keep going. Just like that," he coaxes. "And then it's your turn."

His hips flex into my hand, and as soon as his head falls back, he's coming into the stream of the shower with his fingertips biting the inside of my wrist. Once he lets go and opens his eyes, I feel scorched, as if his green eyes are fire.

Nolan takes a step closer to me and quickly undoes the button of my jeans. He pushes the denim down past my hips, and I kick my shoes off to the bench. I'm in nothing but my panties and damp blue sweater with his come swirling beneath our feet and down the drain.

"Spread, Hannah."

I do as he says.

"And keep your eyes on me the entire time."

THIRTEEN
WET DREAMS

NOLAN

Hannah Evans is what wet dreams are made of.

Her hands fall to my shoulders, and I embrace the way her nails dig into my wet skin.

I hold her steady with one arm around her back, but the other is in between her legs, and I'm toying with her to make the moment last longer.

My mouth skims her ear. "Did you enjoy the show?"

She whimpers out a yes, and I smile. "Do you want to know what I thought of while jerking myself off in front of you?"

Hannah climbs to her tiptoes in a poor attempt to get my hand to move lower. I know where she wants to be touched, and it feels a little bit like an honor for her to not shy away like the last time.

"Ye–yeah," she answers.

"I thought of that pretty little moan from the other night." My teeth sink into her earlobe, and she turns her head to give me more access. I brush a thumb over her clit, and she shivers in my arms. *God.* "And then I thought of what you'll feel like coming on my dick." I smile against her wet neck as the shower continues to rain on top of us. "I can't wait to see you get off with me inside of you."

"You're... so...confident." She's barely able to get the words out.

I rub my thumb against her clit again, but this time, I go hard and fast, and she pushes herself closer to me.

"I am confident. Just look at you letting go for me right now." *It's fucking beautiful.* "I know you haven't gotten off during sex... but tell me," I grip her chin with my free hand and stare at her mouth. "Have you ever gotten off like this for your ex? Have you shown anyone the face you make when you come?" I squeeze her jaw. "And faking it doesn't count."

Our eyes meet, and hers are hooded with lust. They droop with something seductive, and I want to be the one to put that look in her eye over and over again.

Fuck, am I all of a sudden addicted to her?

I slip a finger inside and hook her leg around my bare hip. My dick is hard again, and I know she can feel me pushing against her.

"No," she admits quietly, looking me dead in the eye.

I back her to the tiled wall and finger her a few times before I can't take it anymore. My mouth is on hers, and I'm swallowing every little whimper that climbs from the back of her throat. Our tongues dance against each other, and I feel her everywhere. I bite onto her bottom lip and slip another finger inside of her, hooking it to hit a different spot.

She breaks our kiss, and her head goes into my shoulder.

"Fuck my hand, Hannah." I smirk when she whimpers. *I think she likes it when I talk dirty.* "I want to be the first man to ever watch you come. Give it to me."

Hannah's hips start rolling against my palm, and I press harder to give her clit the push it needs. She's moving quickly, and I watch her pussy swallow my fingers.

"Oh my g—"

I rub my palm against her clit one more time, and she breaks. Her legs go slack, and her eyes shut. I stare at her parted lips, and her moan is a melody to my ears. My fingers push deep inside as her pussy continues to wrap around them to ride out her orgasm. I'm tempted to bring her to another orgasm just so I can watch her again.

"Good girl," I whisper against her ear.

Her entire body shakes in my arms, and when I pull my fingers out, our eyes meet.

"I..." her voice is raspy and her eyes are wide. "I can't believe you got me off."

My lip lifts. "Looks like we both earned an A."

FOURTEEN
GET OUT OF MY HEAD, NOLAN

HANNAH

I've been to thousands of hockey games over the years.

With an older brother playing hockey since I was barely old enough to walk, I've lived most of my life at the rink.

However, Wilder U's hockey games are the rowdiest I've ever been to. The student section is so loud and rambunctious that even Aria is perplexed.

"You weren't kidding!" she shouts into my ear. "I'm even more excited to start attending Wilder U now."

I laugh while keeping my eyes on the game. Hayes has already gotten two points, and both assists were from Nolan, which is really no surprise. I'm beginning to understand that Nolan is a force to be reckoned with—on and off the ice.

"And..." Aria gets closer to me. "This game is totally worth driving back to EC at midnight tonight so I can catch my shift in the morning."

"I vote you stay with me and just call off."

Aria shakes her head. "I can't. I have to save enough so we can live lavishly when I transfer."

"If eating ramen and using Hayes's Netflix subscription is living lavishly, well then...okay."

We both laugh and continue to watch the game. There are a few girls that I know from classes in front of me, and when they keep peeking back, Aria finally asks them what they're looking at.

"Sorry," one of them squeaks. Her cheeks have too much blush, and her glossy blue eyes sparkle under the lights, telling everyone who looks at her that she's had too many beers. "We aren't gawking at you two. It's just..." She looks past my head, and I turn to see the spectacle.

I freeze instantly—as if Reign Kendrix somehow knows that my best friend looked him up and told me that I should try dating him so I can *practice* having sex.

Reign sees me staring, but I quickly turn away, pretending like I have no idea who he is. In an attempt to disengage, I shout to Aria, "I'm gonna go get another beer. Want one?"

"No, I'm good. I gotta drive. Want me to come with?"

"No, keep rooting our boys on. If they lose, Hayes will throw a hissy."

As soon as I make it to the steps and turn around, I nearly fall backward from the massive boulder standing in my way. His palm finds my lower back, and his voice is smoother than the glass at my back.

"Careful."

Reign Kendrix is towering over me, and by the look in his eye, I know the rumors around campus are true. He is full of sex appeal. The warm grin he's sporting doesn't fool me one bit.

"Thanks." I try to move around him, but he meets me halfway. I hitch an eyebrow and try to seem confident, although I'm anything but. "Um, excuse me?"

"Here." I look down at his hand, and he's holding a beer out for me. I pull back with surprise. "I heard you say you were going to go get a beer, but the line is crazy long. I got an extra when I went up a little while ago. I think it's still cold."

I'm confused by the gesture but also slightly swayed by his generosity. "Oh. Are you sure?"

"Yes," he chuckles. "I'm always sure."

I lightly laugh. "Well, thank you?" *Why is he handing me a beer?*

When I go to turn back to my aisle, he steps in my way and steals my attention. "Who are you?"

I furrow my eyebrows. "Uh..." I laugh softly. "No one, really."

Reign's eyebrows shoot to his hairline. "I beg to differ."

"That's Hayes Evans's sister," someone says from behind.

My cheeks grow warm.. As soon as I moved into Hayes's apartment and the hockey team learned who I was, I have been noticed a lot more around campus than before.

Reign nods. "Gotcha. That explains why you're rooting for him." He smiles. "I thought he may be your boyfriend."

I make a face. "Ew."

He chuckles and I give him a look. "Wait. If you thought I was his girlfriend, why did you give me your beer? Do you have some feud with my brother and want to piss him off?"

"What? No." He looks appalled. "I'm here to support the hockey team. I don't have a feud with anyone." Reign looks past my shoulder at the ice. "I gave you my beer to be kind and maybe because I wanted to see if you were taken."

"She isn't!" Aria shouts from our seats.

I send her a scathing look. I swear, if she somehow got

ahold of Reign and told him to ask me out, I'm going to end our friendship.

I shake my head. "I'm not taken..." *Why is Nolan suddenly in my head?* "But I'm not really looking for anything serious right now."

Reign shrugs. "Me either. But maybe we can sit together at the next game? You can pay me back for the beer." He winks, and there's a little tug in my chest.

"Okay," I finally say. "I'll sit with you at the next game, but we'll see about the beer."

He smiles, and I realize that he is just as handsome up close as he is on the football field. Dark hair, bright-green eyes, thick black eyelashes. Total opposite of Nolan's sandy hair and golden-boy looks. *Wait. Get out of my head, Nolan.*

"What's your number?"

I rattle the digits off to him and feel a text come in a second later, but before I can open my phone, I jump from the loud sound at my back. The beer Reign gave me spills out from the top when I spin to see the commotion.

My chest tightens when I catch Nolan staring *right* at me. He has an opposing player pinned to the glass with an arm pressed to his windpipe, but for some reason, his gaze is set directly on me.

It takes my brother coming up behind him to snatch his jersey and skate him off to the side for him to finally look away. I watch as the ref throws Nolan into the sin bin, and I can't help but wonder what set him off in the first place.

Reign's warm breath tingles my neck when he leans down to whisper in my ear. "Well, now you owe me two beers."

I laugh lightly and shake my head, making my way back to Aria and her knowing little grin.

FIFTEEN
IN THE DEEP END

NOLAN

I haven't cracked a smile in at least twenty-four hours, which wouldn't be noticeable if we had lost our game, but we won by three, so I truly have no good excuse for my stoicism.

Van throws a pizza crust at my head, and the girl on his lap giggles. I catch it with my sharp reflexes and glare.

"Bro, what is your deal? Need this one to call a friend over for you or something?"

Hayes laughs under his breath as he rests against the couch. He's been buried in his phone the entire evening, which is to my benefit because at least he can't see me watching his sister from across the room.

A loud clanking noise comes from the kitchen, and I glance up to see Hannah looking directly at me. The moment we make eye contact, she goes back to doing the dishes and pretending like she wasn't paying attention to what my answer may be.

The smallest amount of jealousy is still swarming my veins from watching her interact with Reign at the game last night. I was impulsive and threw a mouthy player up against the glass to get her attention. *What was I thinking?* I can't wrap my head around it, and I'm agitated because of it.

"Depends." I look at Van and his girl. "What's she look like?"

"Shallow much?" I whip my head toward Hannah and flex my jaw. *She has some nerve.*

Hayes cackles but quickly comes to my rescue. "Of course we're shallow. It's not like we're looking for anything serious. She doesn't need to be the type to bring home to Mom. We're looking to get laid and nothing more."

Hannah's mouth flies open. Then a wet towel flies from her grip and lands on Hayes's head. "You're a pig, Hayes!"

He shrugs. "I'm allowed to be."

"What would you say if *I* were that type of girl? The kind that is looking to get laid and nothing more?"

Hayes closes his mouth after looking disgusted. I can't even look at her because, to me, she kind of *is* that girl. I swear my fingers tingle with the thought of where they were a few nights prior.

"You're not that type, so don't even act like you are."

Hannah's cheeks flare with heat, and when she looks over at me, time stops.

Fuck, don't look at me.

I gulp and look away. I finally get the nerve to direct my attention to Hayes. "I thought you were going to a party?"

"Yeah, I am. And you're coming." He stands, along with Van and the girl on his lap. They start to gather their things, and it feels like someone just stole the puck from me and scored the opposite goal. They're waiting for me, and I don't have a valid excuse not to go.

I skim past Van's hand on his date's hip and briefly

make eye contact with Hannah. I can't deny the pull I feel when I look at her, but I also know that my excuse to stay back so I can be alone with her isn't going to fly, so I give up.

"Alright, whatever. But I'm not staying long."

Van laughs. "You say that every single time, and every single time, you are one of the last to leave."

"With hickeys on your neck, no less." Hayes wiggles his eyebrows, and I hate that he's right. I also hate that I want to clock him for saying that in front of his sister.

Why do I care?

"Let's go." I head for the door, refusing to look at Hannah again.

Our agreement is simple. I teach her some basic skills in the bedroom, and she goes on a date with Reign, or whoever else she wants, with a little more confidence. If I need a favor, she'll cash it in. That's it. There is nothing else about it.

But tell me why it feels wrong to go to a party instead of staying at home with her?

SIXTEEN
ONCE YOU'RE HIS, YOU'RE NO LONGER MINE

HANNAH

It's late when the door opens.

I haven't been asleep long, but I'm groggy enough to keep my eyes closed when footsteps walk past the couch and into the kitchen, then down the hall and into a room.

It sounded like one set of feet, but it could have been any one of the guys. It doesn't mean it was Nolan, and it doesn't mean that he came home early instead of getting *hickeys* at a party.

I sigh and turn to my side.

Ever since the locker room, I've been left feeling like I need *more*. Every time I look at Nolan's hands, whether he's holding a fork, or a glass of water, or typing a text on his phone, I can't help but want them in between my legs.

It's a sickness and all the more reason why I need to actually go forward with the *non-date* with Reign. According to Aria, him asking me to sit with him at the next game is a date that can definitely lead to more, but I'm not sure I see it that way.

Regardless, I need to go forward with it.

Even if it doesn't go beyond the game, at least Nolan proved to me that I *can* get off in front of someone other than myself. He's already helped me more than he knows.

My phone vibrates on the table beside the couch, and I reach up to grab it. My eyes squint at the brightness.

> Teach: Are you actually asleep, or are you pretending so you can avoid me?

My heart races, and excitement bubbles in my lower belly like I've chugged an entire bottle of wine.

> Me: I should be surprised that you put yourself in my phone as Teach, but I'm not.

> Teach: Well, if you're up, what are you waiting for? We have a lesson to get to.

> Me: If you think I want your hands on me after you've been touching some other girl at a party, you're wrong.

I swallow a bitter pill and pretend it isn't jealousy.

> Teach: The only girl I want to touch tonight is you. Why do you think I'm home before everyone else?

A smile falls to my lips, which is nothing more than a giant red warning, but instead of heeding it, I put my blinders on.

> Me: And if my brother comes home?

> Teach: Then I guess I'll have to teach you how to be quiet.

The hot twisting is already present, and I'm not even in the same room as him. He texts me again before I can type anything back.

> Teach: I saw you talking to Reign at the game, which means we're running out of time for lessons. Once you're his, you're no longer mine.

> Me: So you think I'm yours?

I click my phone screen off when I hear his door open. My heart is in my throat, and I cross my legs to ignore the heat. Nolan's footsteps are steady, and although it's completely dark in the apartment, I can see his tall shadow standing only a few feet away from the couch.

"You may not be mine," he says with a low voice, "but for now, your body is. So, let's go, Hannah."

I flush from my head to my toes. Nolan bends down and pulls the blanket off my legs, and I stand up. I'm prepared to follow him to his room, but he quickly grips me under the butt and picks me up, wrapping my legs around his back.

Not a single word is spoken until we're in his room and the door shuts.

When my feet hit the floor, he strips out of his shirt and throws it off to the side.

"Lock the door, and then get on the bed."

SEVENTEEN
TRAPPED

NOLAN

I'm out of my ever-loving mind.

Hannah is pulling things out of my subconscious at this point.

Her body is mine? I actually told her that her body was mine, and as soon as I said it, I expected her to blanch. To my surprise, she didn't. Instead, she stood up and was fully ready to give me more.

I went to the party with her brother and Van, and although a handful of girls came up to me, asking to dance—and *other* things—the only thing I could think of was leaving so I could get home to her.

There's a chemistry that I feel with Hannah that I haven't felt with anyone before, and the more I'm with her, the stronger it becomes.

What the fuck is happening?

I ignore the thought as I stare at her on top of my covers. Her brown hair spills out around her head as she lies on the pillow, and although I should just finish this whole thing between us, I want to take it slower so I selfishly have more moments with her.

The bed dips when I climb on top and settle between her legs. My desk lamp is the only light in the room, and it gives off just enough of a glow that I can see her pretty blue eyes twinkle with anticipation.

"Tell me," I lower my voice when I push her shirt up to expose her belly. "Has anyone tasted you before?"

Her eyes widen briefly before she shifts them away from my face.

"Eyes on me, Hannah."

Our gazes catch. "Yes."

I raise an eyebrow as I push her shirt up even higher, showing off the rounded undersides of her breasts. *Fuck, no bra.* "But?"

She laughs. "It wasn't very good."

Well, isn't she in for a ride, then?

"Meaning they didn't even come close to getting you off?"

She nods slowly. A sharp inhale escapes when I dip my head to her belly and place soft kisses all the way up to the hem of her shirt. I push the cotton higher and almost die at the sight of her perky nipple. I take it in my mouth, and her back arches.

I pull back and shove her little sleep shorts down past her hips. "I bet you got them off, though, didn't you?" I reach up and place my thumb on her soft bottom lip and rub it gently. "From the way you kiss, I know that mouth is talented."

A quick nod is all I get in response.

"Well, baby, I have no problem paying you back for all the times you weren't rewarded."

Hannah's hands grip my covers. I blow hot puffs of air

against her clit before flicking my tongue and rubbing it against her tight little seam. Her knuckles turn white when she grabs my comforter even tighter, and I smile against her pussy.

She tastes better than I imagined, and when I tell her to spread, she follows my command without hesitation. I lick, suck, and nip on every part of her until she's squirming beneath me.

"Nolan." My name is a sexy breath falling off her lips, and I know I'm teasing her more than I should, but I'm not in the mood to rush through this. She tastes too good, and getting her off when no man ever has...it's too fucking rewarding. *I get all her firsts.*

"I'll let you come," I say against her clit, "but first, tell me what you want."

"More," she demands, tilting her hips to my face.

"Good girl. That's more like it. Don't be afraid to tell someone what you want." I bite gently before releasing her clit and sucking. I put a finger inside her, and she moans at the pleasure. Her hot, tight walls clamp onto me, and it forces me to get her off because I can't help but crave more of that sound coming from her mouth.

"Fuck," I whisper at the sound coming from the apartment. "Hurry and be quiet."

The shutting of the front door is hardly loud enough to make it to my bedroom, but I knew Van and Hayes would be coming home sooner or later, and they picked the worst possible time.

"I...I can't." She's panicking.

"Yes, you can, Han. Focus on what I'm doing to you and nothing else. I'll keep you quiet."

Why is it so fulfilling for me to pleasure her *and* take care of her?

My heart thumps painfully, and when I suck a little harder on her clit and pinch her nipple, I feel the orgasm against my fingers. I slap my other hand over her mouth. "Bite down."

Her teeth sink into my palm, and something wickedly hot rushes right to my dick. *Fuck me.*

The way her hips move against my face is purely seductive, and it feels like a trap.

Hannah has me pinned, and I'm not talking about her knees pressed against my ears.

EIGHTEEN
ONE LESSON WASN'T ENOUGH

HANNAH

"Go," he urges, opening the door and peeking down the dark hallway.

I slip past him, but his hand wraps around my waist as the last second, and he pulls me back. I land against his chest, and my hair flies past my face. One second, I'm confused, and the next, I'm consumed. Nolan's mouth works over mine slowly but deeply with his hand cupped against my cheek and tangled in my hair.

I breathe in the charged air in cupfuls.

"'Night, Hannah," he whispers, gently pushing me out the door.

I can't manage to say anything back to him. I'm too jarred by his gentle touch and lingering kiss.

Things feel different.

My body is sated, but my heart is jumbled.

There's a distinct pull in my chest, and I'm too flustered to decipher what it is, even after I lie on the couch for an hour, tossing and turning.

I nibble on my thumb and try to fall asleep, but every time I close my eyes, all I can think about is Nolan.

Nolan's mouth.

Nolan's cheeky smile.

Nolan's quick gaze when I enter the room.

Nolan's low voice in the dark, coaxing me to break for him.

Damnit.

This isn't good.

The orgasms are messing with my head.

I flop onto my back and sigh. My hair blows past my face, and I focus on Reign instead, in an attempt to push the feelings I'm conflicted over onto someone else.

Sadly, it doesn't work.

The blanket flies to the floor, and I swing my legs to stand. My bare feet pad silently against the creaky wood, and I'm not even standing in front of Nolan's door for two seconds before it opens. He's standing there in nothing but low-riding sweatpants and his taunting abs.

He's surprised one second, but the next, he's pulling me inside and locking the door.

We stare at each other, but neither one of us says anything.

My heart skips when he takes a step toward me. He furrows his heavy brow-line for a fleeting second before placing his hands on both sides of my face and tilting my mouth to his.

I exhale a breath of relief when he kisses me, like there was no way I'd survive the night without it.

I ignore the thought and kiss him back.

My hands gingerly touch his waist, and he backs us up until he's sitting on his bed, and I'm straddling his lap.

"What made you come back for more?" he whispers against my mouth.

His hands are holding my waist in place as my hair falls around us like a shield.

"I don't know," I say, edging closer to him.

"One lesson wasn't enough?" he jokes. I know it's an attempt to lighten the heaviness that's silently behind our lustful touches, but it doesn't work.

I gulp, and he pulls me in closer.

I go in for another kiss, and this time, it's full of hunger.

Nolan's tongue whips against mine, and the smallest moan slips from the back of my throat. I move over his sweats, and he curses under his breath.

"*Fuck*. You're addicting, Han."

My shirt is thrown onto the floor, and my hair tumbles down my back when he moves his lips to my jaw. He places featherlight kisses there and down the side of my neck, sending goosebumps to my flesh. I thrust my chest into his face, and he buries his nose before inhaling deeply, as if he loves my scent.

"Up," he hisses.

I sit straighter, and his sweats are off and discarded near my shirt. Then comes my shorts and panties, and suddenly, we're both bare, and there isn't a single thing separating us.

The way I'm moving against him and the way he can't stop touching every part of my body doesn't feel like some lesson he conjured up.

Our touches are passionate, and from the outside looking in, we seem uncontrollable.

Nolan's hand falls to his hard length, and I look down once before meeting his hooded gaze. My hand disappears in his thick, sandy hair, and when he positions himself, I slowly slide down and bite my lower lip until I'm so full I stop breathing.

"*Perfect,*" he whispers. "Are you on birth control?"

He tilts his hips, and I gasp out a '*yes.*'

The way Nolan moves in and out of me, all while keeping my hips steady, makes me tingle all over. I feel an orgasm peaking, and I think he can feel it too, because he keeps still and lets me move against him the way I want to.

"That's it, baby." He pulls on my hair, and my head goes back with the tug. I shut my eyes when his mouth descends on my neck. "Get off for me."

I move faster and roll my hips to hit the spot that he's making sure to keep a hold of. My mouth opens, and a breathless moan clamors out. He catches it with his and pushes up to meet me halfway. I completely lose myself and chase the orgasm.

"Jesus Christ." Nolan's fingers dig into my curves, and in the midst of orgasming, he pushes up one more time to hit a spot that has my heart stopping. Then, he flips me onto the bed, and his come spills all over my stomach.

We both stare at the mess he's made before making eye contact. My mouth stays open with shock, even while he cleans me up. After he throws the towel off to the side and helps me get dressed, he pulls me back to the bed, and we lie there in calm silence.

I don't know how much time has passed when I feel him pick me up. I press my check into his chest in my sleepy state, and he carries me through the dark apartment and back to the couch.

The pad of his thumb trails down the side of my cheek before he rests it on my lip.

And then he turns and heads back to his room before

my brother finds out that his best friend and teammate just showed his sister what it's like to be worshiped in the bedroom.

NINETEEN
HERS

NOLAN

I no longer want to be called Teach.

Instead, I want to be called *hers*.

I'm in deep fucking shit. I can't even look in Hannah's direction without bursting at the seams, and for once, I'm not referring to my dick. My best friend's little sister has somehow turned my entire world upside down with just a few stolen moments behind closed doors.

The hockey puck flies into the net when I hit one after another during warmups. My muscles are tight, and my eyes dart to the stands every couple of minutes, wondering if Hannah is going to stay true to her word and show up with Wilder U's quarterback beside her.

I heard her talking to her best friend on the phone. Neither one of them seems to remember that anyone within earshot will overhear their conversation. Or maybe Hannah wanted me to hear her conversation.

"Are you going to sit with Reign tonight?"

"Well, yeah. It would be awkward if he picked me up and I ended up sitting somewhere else."

"He's picking you up too? I was right. It's totally a date!"

"I don't know if I want it to be a date..."

"What? Why?"

"I...I don't know."

She hesitated, and I wanted her next words to be, *"Because I'm interested in Nolan."* But they weren't, because why would they be? We've been sneaking around the apartment for weeks, and I'm nothing more than her mentor. I volunteered to secretly help her gain confidence in the bedroom, and that was it. I've given her no indication otherwise, and who would ever expect it? I have never even been seen with the same girl more than once.

I mean, hell, I can't believe the thoughts rolling around my head.

"Dude, is that your sister with Reign Kendrix?"

Hayes and I both turn at the same time. My teeth crack together as my teammates skate zig-zags around us. Hayes turns to me with a *what-the-fuck* look on his face, like I'm supposed to answer for her actions.

"That's who she was talking about with Aria?"

I shrug to hide my irritation. "How would I know?"

Hayes squints at my gruff tone. "Because I saw you listening to her conversation right before I started to listen."

I turn and skate away, trying to keep my eyes from going in her direction, which is a struggle during warmups that later leads into the first period.

I chug some water but stare up into the stands past my water bottle. Hannah has her brown hair pulled back, and she's laughing at something Reign has said. I huff before turning my back to them.

Van elbows me from beside the bench.

"What?" I snap.

"If you want her, go get her."

I feel like I've been caught red-handed. My jaw flickers with irritation.

"What the fuck are you talking about?"

Van laughs loudly and draws the attention of the entire team. "Look at you, all pissy and throwing a tantrum on the ice. Just go tell Hayes that you're fucking his sister, and run up there and tell her. Then maybe we'll win the game with your head out of your ass."

I stare at Van before turning away and contemplating his half-ass advice.

If there has ever been an obstacle in my way of getting what I want, I demolish it. Like I said before, I like a challenge, and what the hell am I doing letting someone like her get away?

I want her.

I want her so much that I'm allowing it to bleed onto the ice during the game. That has to mean something, right?

Three minutes until we're due back in the rink.

Three minutes to risk it all for something that may not even work.

Before I can rethink it, I move down a few spots on the bench and stand in front of Hayes. He's mid-conversation with our right winger when he glances up.

"What's up?"

He's hyped on the game, with adrenaline pumping through his veins, and my only hope is that he doesn't use that adrenaline to deck me in the face.

It's always better to ask forgiveness than to ask for permission.

I clear my throat, look him dead in the face, and apologize. "I'm sorry."

"For what?" he asks.

I turn and make my way over to the glass below the student section and pretend I don't hear Hayes behind me.

"Did you fuck my sister, Nolan? I swear to God."

The entire row of my teammates gasps in between a few snickers. Coach's voice catches my ear. "Jesus Christ. *Guys!* Come on!"

My fist bangs on the clear barrier, and everyone turns to look. Hannah's blue eyes widen, and I lift my finger and hook it toward myself. "Come here," I mouth.

Reign looks between us, and Hannah's face couldn't be redder.

"Now."

I pull my helmet off and shake out my sweaty hair.

The attention is on us. Everything silences when she descends down the steps and crosses her arms over her Wilder U sweatshirt. "What are you doing?" she seethes. She's obviously bothered by the stares, but the only thing I can focus on is her.

The glass isn't super thick, but I make sure everyone can hear me.

"Remember when I said you owed me a favor?"

Hannah rolls her eyes and looks around at everyone staring. Shit, even my coach is staring. "You want to cash in your favor right now? In the middle of a game?!"

My mouth twitches. "Yes."

Hannah glares. "Fine. What's the favor? What do you want me to do, Nolan?"

I point past her head at Reign. I have nothing against the guy, but she's mine. "Tell your little boyfriend up there that you're taken."

Shock and confusion flicker across her face. "What?!"

"You have to tell him that you're taken."

"That's not a favor! That's—"

"What I want," I finish for her. "You owe me, Hannah."

She thinks for a moment and glances at her brother off to the side. I pull her attention back by tapping on the glass.

"I have another request."

The buzzer sounds, and I know it's time for me to get back on the ice.

"Okay, what?" she hurries, knowing I have to get back to the game.

"I want you to be mine."

Her mouth opens before she snaps it shut, only to open it again. "Wh–what? But we're... You..."

"Yes or no, Hannah?"

Hayes skates past. "For fuck's sake, just say yes! We have a game to play!" he shouts over his shoulder. "I'm fucking pissed at you, Nolan."

Hannah laughs abruptly and shows off her rosy-red cheeks. I raise an eyebrow, waiting for her answer, and when she can't hold back a smile, I know she's about to become mine.

"Fine." She waves her hand toward the ice. "Now go win the game, and maybe Hayes won't kill you after!"

I pull my mask down and grin.

It would be worth it.

AFTERWORD

If you enjoyed this fast-paced, spicy lessons novella that takes place at Wilder U, make sure to check my website for updates on on the first book in the series!

sjsylvis.com

ALSO BY SJ SYLVIS
BEXLEY U SERIES

Bexley U Series
Weak Side
Ice Bet
Puck Block

Chicago Blue Devils
Play the Game
Skate the Line
Rush the Edge

Wilder U
Untitled (coming soon!)

Shadow Valley Series
Sticks and Stones
Heart of Thorns
Untitled (releasing 12/2025)

English Prep Series
All the Little Lies

All the Little Secrets
All the Little Truths

St. Mary's Series
Good Girls Never Rise
Bad Boys Never Fall
Dead Girls Never Talk
Heartless Boys Never Kiss
Pretty Girls Never Lie

Standalones
Three Summers
Yours Truly, Cammie
Chasing Ivy
Falling for Fallon
Truth

ABOUT THE AUTHOR

S.J. Sylvis is an Amazon top 50 and USA Today bestselling author who is best known for her new adult sport romances. She currently resides in Arizona with her husband, two small children, dog and cat! She is obsessed with coffee, becomes easily attached to fictional characters, and spends most of her evenings buried in a book!

Stay up to date at: sjsylvis.com

Made in United States
Troutdale, OR
05/08/2025

31193162R00059